Sticky
Graphic
Novels
NIGHTLIFE

NIGHTLIFE

©2009 Dale Lazarov, Bastian Jonsson & Yann Duminil
// All rights reserved.

StickyGraphicNovels.com

Printed and distributed by
ComicMix, LLC.
71 Hauxhurst Ave. Suite B
Weehawken, NJ 07086.
http://www.comicmix.com

Printed in USA.

Hardcover ISBN: 9781939888709

"Hard Cases"

THE
TAILPIECE
BAR
Tonight:
Open Mike

BOOBS
ASS

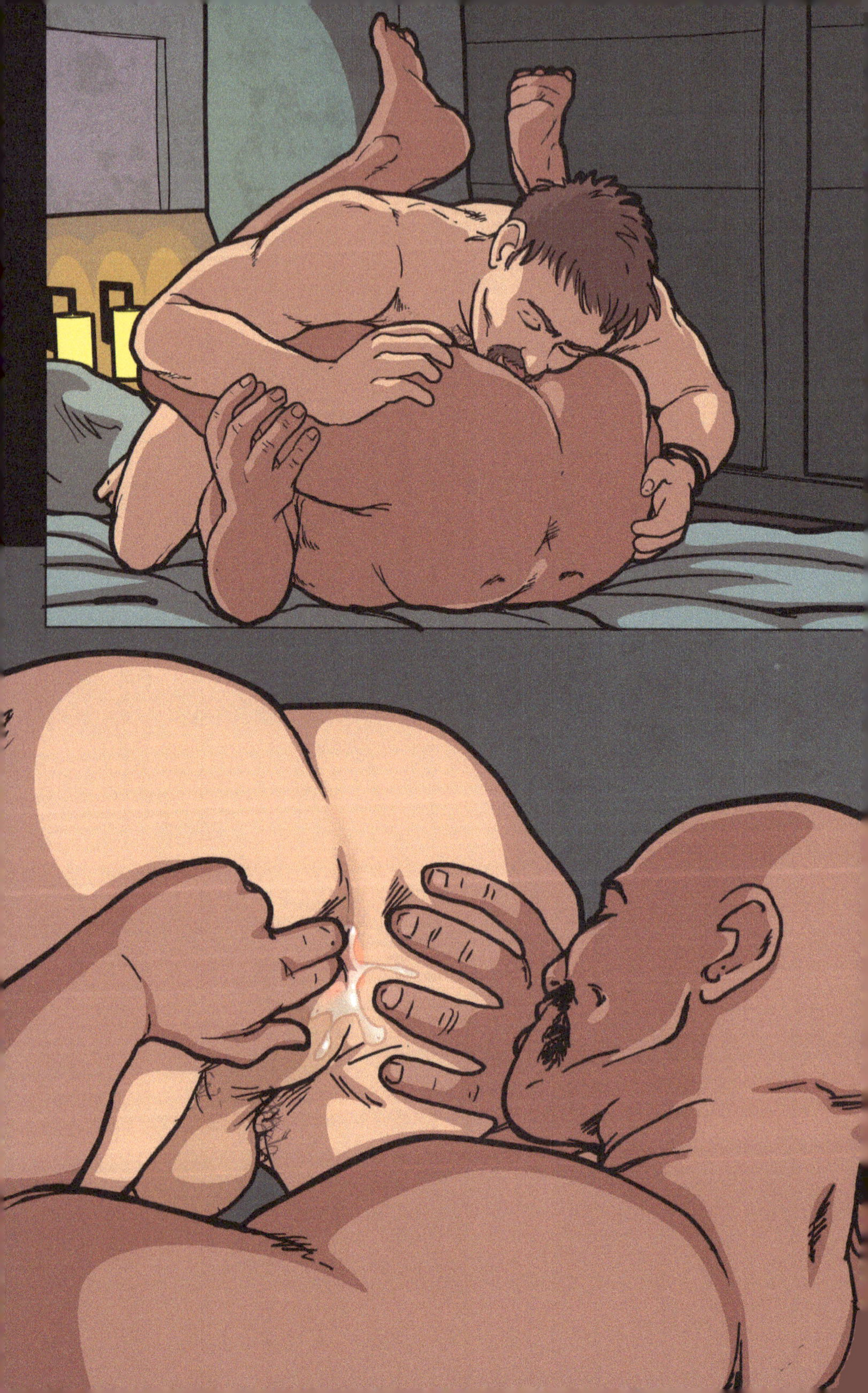

BIG BOY

TITS
BOOTY

"Layover"

B04 19:32 CANCELLE
B29 19:36 CANCELLE
A34 19:39 CANCELLE
B32 19:41 CANCELLE
C23 19:44 CANCELLE
A06 19:45 CANCELLE
A32 19:48 CANCELLE
B21 19:51 CANCELLE
C34 19:53 CANCELLE

Hotel

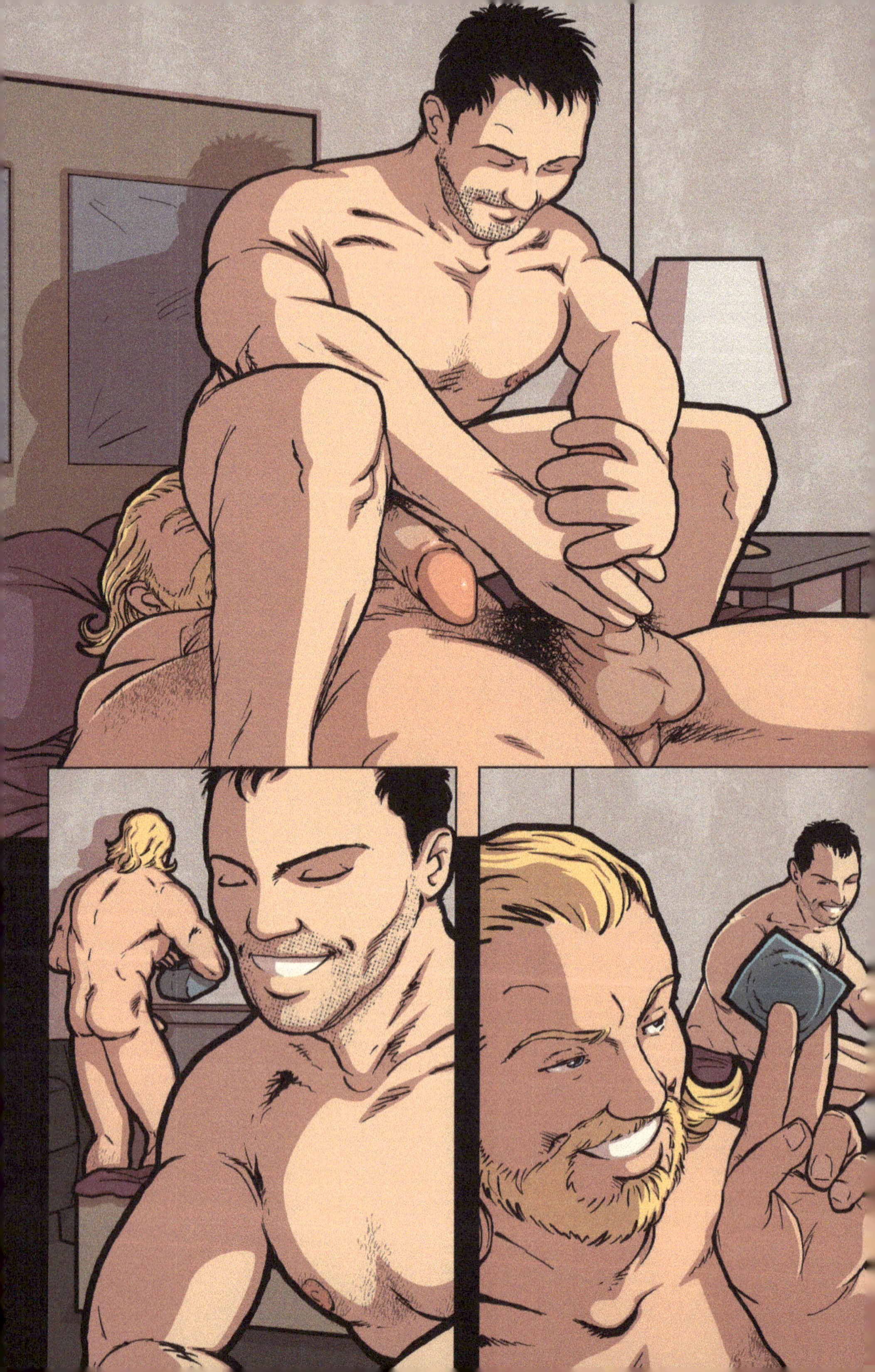

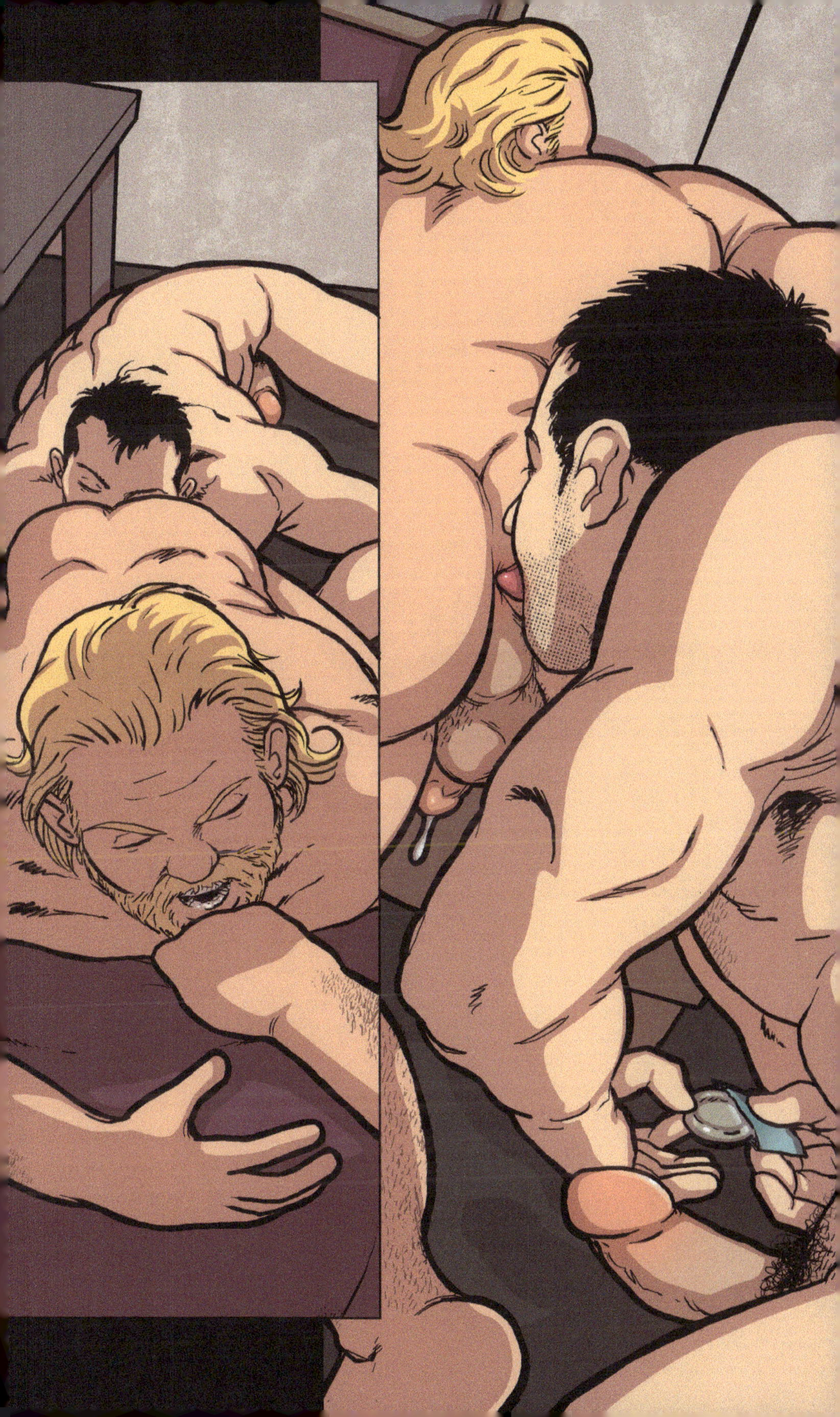

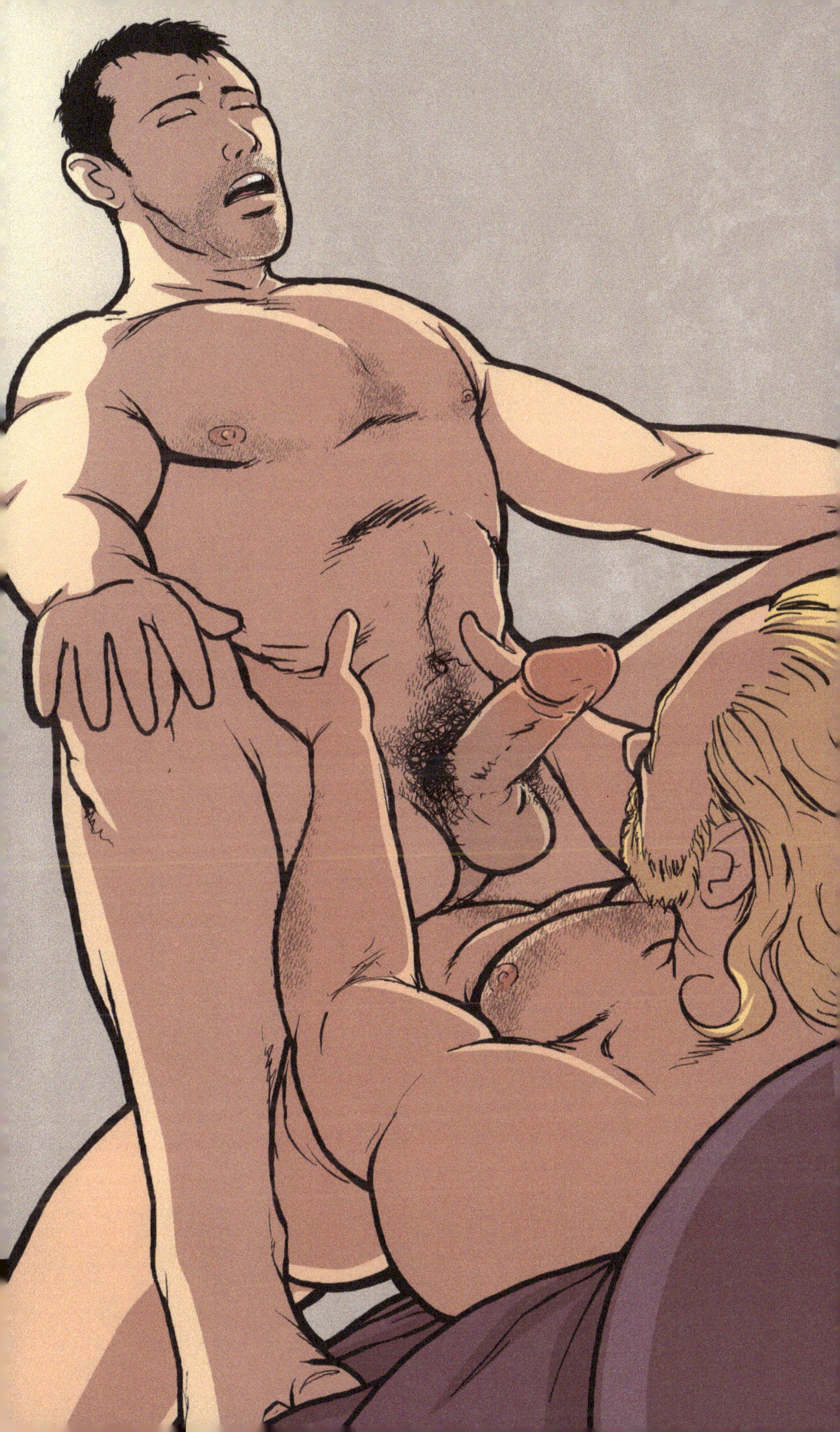

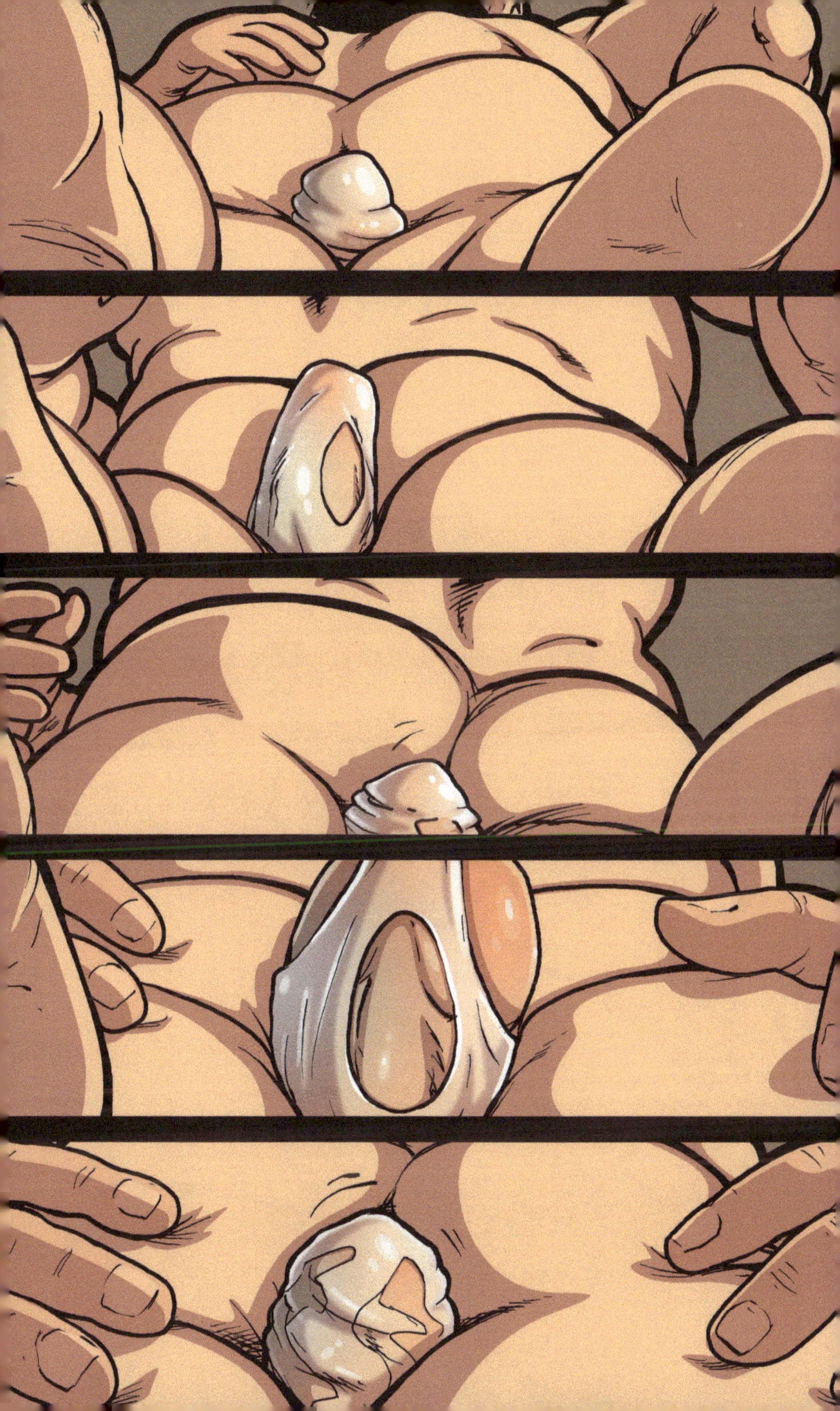

07:00

"Closing Time"

Salvation

L&F

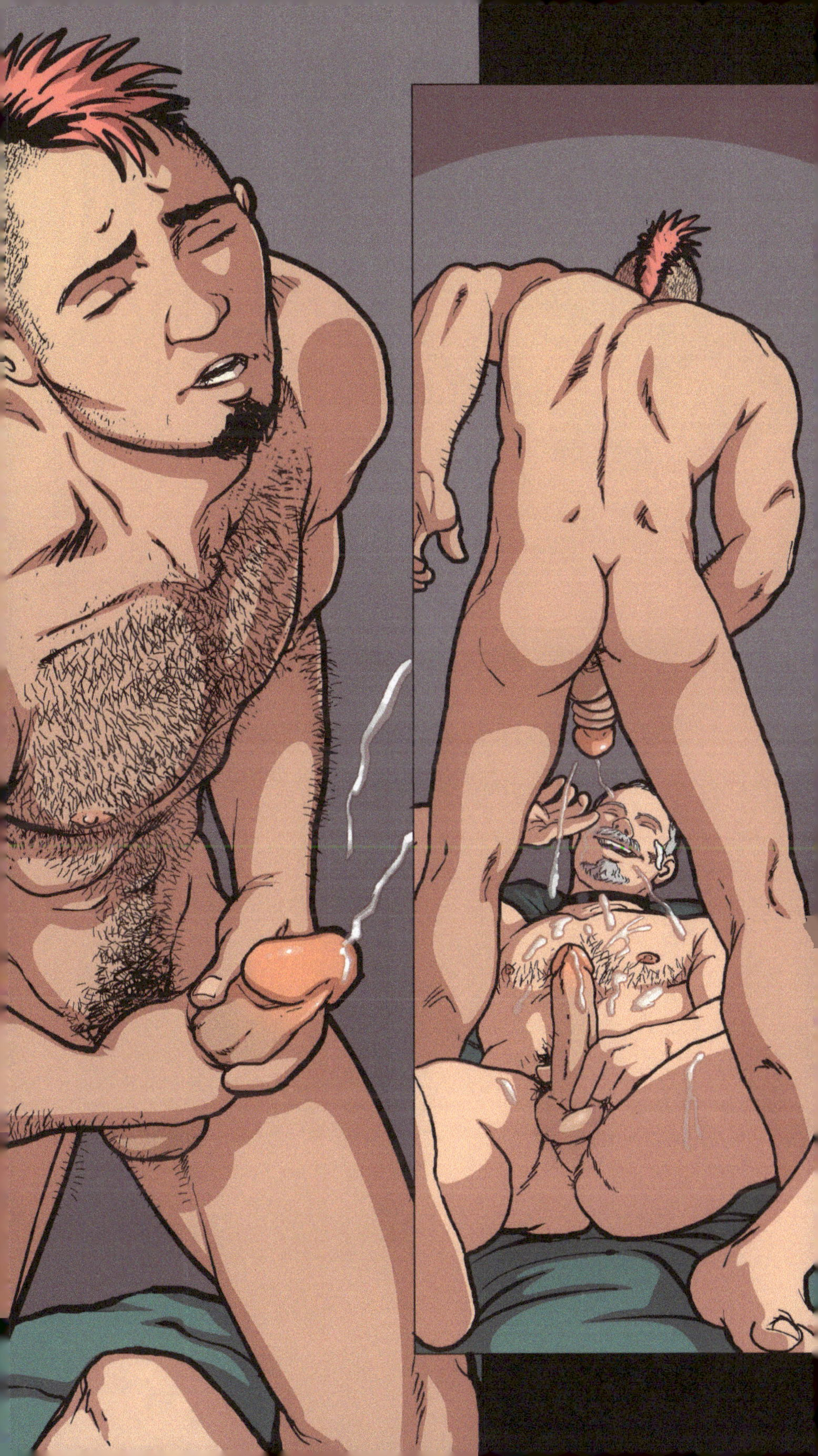

script/edits: Dale Lazarov
line art: Bastian Jonsson
color art: Yann Duminil

About The Authors:

Dale Lazarov is known as The Father of American Bara Comics as the writer, art director and licensor of Sticky Graphic Novels. Sticky Graphic Novels are wordless, gay character-based, sex-positive graphic novels for an international audience that are considered "a joyous expression of male/male sexuality that, while erotic, is neither grubby nor tasteless" (*The Novel Approach*). Since 2006, he has collaborated on 15 hardcover Sticky Graphic Novels and 41 digital editions with distinctive and evocative gay comics artists from around the globe. In his secret identity, he is Aldo Alvarez, Ph.D., and lives in Chicago.

Bastian Jonsson specialises in illustration, graphic design, communication and PR, and lives in a very small town nestled in the endless, moose-infested forests of rural west Sweden, with his long-suffering veterinary husband, a very spoiled dog and far, far too many horses.

Yann Duminil trained as an illustrator at the Emile Cohl Drawing School, in Lyon, France. After earning a degree in Illustration and Comics, he returned to Nice to begin his illustration career (and go to the beach). After working for two years in a creative agency as a graphi, he went freelance in 2002. He's done many illustrations for advertising and the press as well as flash games, cartoons and web design. He now lives and works near Paris with his boyfriend and their overweight but cute cat, Stitch.